VICTOR MONTEJO

translated by Wallace Kaufman

THE BIRD WHO
CLEANS
THE WORLD
and other Mayan Fables

CURBSTONE PRESS

Cover design by Stone Graphics
Printed in the U.S. by BookCrafters

Some of these fables were previously published in *International Wildlife*
(January/February 1984), *Bomb* (Spring/Summer 1985), *Indian Studies*
(Vol. 1, No. 2 May/ June 1984. Cornell University), *Mesoamerica*
(Vol 10, 1985.), *Bucknell World* (Vol. 14, No. 4 May 1985), and *The
Carrillon* (Fall 1988).

These Mayan fables were also used to illustrate Victor Montejo's M.A.
Thesis, *Oral Tradition: An Anthropological Study of a Jakaltek Folktale*,
(Ms.) SUNY, Albany (1989).

Curbstone Press is a 501(c)(3) nonprofit literary arts organization
whose operations are supported in part by private donations and by
grants from the ADCO Foundation, the Bissel Foundation, the
Connecticut Commission on the Arts, the LEF Foundation, the Lila
Wallace-Readers Digest Fund, the Andrew W. Mellon Foundation, the
National Endowment for the Arts, and the Plumsock Fund.

This publication received project support from The National
Endowment for the Arts and the Connecticut Commission on the Arts,
a state agency whose funds are recommended by the Governor and
appropriated by the State Legislature.

ISBN; 1-880684-03-9
Library of Congress number: 90-52757

distributed in the US by
INBOOK

published by
Curbstone Press
321 Jackson Street
Willimantic, CT 06226

A Linguistic Note

These Mayan fables and animal stories were collected
and transcribed by the author from Jakaltek-Maya
language, one of the 21 Mayan languages that are
still spoken in Guatemala.

Names that are provided in Jakaltek-Maya in
this volume, are written following the graphemes of
the official alphabet of Mayan Languages elaborated
by the Academia de las Lenguas Mayas de
Guatemala (Academy of Mayan Languages), for the
purpose of standardizing the practice of writing
Mayan languages with Latin characters.

contents

I dedicate this book to my mother, Juana Esteban Méndez, and my father, Eusebio Montejo, wonderful storytellers. They have given me the chance to experience both Mayan and non-Mayan world views and ways of life.

To my children: E. Marvin, E. Marilyn, and Victor Ivan Montejo, to whom I particularly dedicate these Mayan fables and stories.

Also, to the elders and storytellers of Jacaltenango, a beautiful town in the Kuchumatanes highlands where I lived my childhood and experienced the Mayan way of life and learning.

Author's Preface

When I was a boy I was always delighted to listen to my mother whenever she wanted to tell me animal stories. Some, she insisted, were true stories from the past, closely related to the Mayan way of life. During my adolescence, my mother continued to tell me the same stories but I tended to forget them easily. As a boy, living in an ever changing world, I could not hold them in my memory as she had done for the decades since her own parents and grandparents told her these stories. She maintained the tradition with care because she feared that these stories that delighted her and other Mayan children in the past would vanish some day because of our carelessness. I always paid attention to my mother. I truly enjoyed her stories, but whenever I laughed because of some of the rationales of the stories, she scolded me by saying: "The young people of today do not believe in their Mayan heritage. That is why they cannot understand and value them."

For my mother, the teachings of the grandmothers and grandfathers and the village elders have intrinsic values and powerful meanings. It does not matter what the story is, you can always interpret its message. Dreams, for example, can foretell the future and are used to interpret events yet to come. Or there are some secret signs that Mayan people read in the behavior of animals or natural elements. Thus, if a *Zip x-Ahaw* (coral snake) appears inside the house behind the water jar, this is a message of death or impending tragedy in the family. If the wood fire in the kitchen whistles under a cooking pot, this predicts a surprise visit. If you dream of dark water gushing from arid places, this is a sign of flood or, depending on the time of the dream, the opposite sign, a drought. All these kinds of stories were taught to my mother by her grandfather. All are intimately linked to our ancestral culture. People, then, must know how to read and interpret those natural and supernatural events that can affect a human's life. They must learn to respect and appreciate those animals and plants that are closely related to our human existence, agriculture and religion.

During my childhood, whenever I wanted to listen to my mother telling Mayan stories, I brought my small chair close to the kitchen fire where she cooked the tortillas, pleading: "Mother, let's tell stories again. Please tell me the story of the injured little dove." Then, my mother would laugh. This is the first story that I remember her telling me, and she knew that I liked her stories very much. So, while the firewood burned under the *comal* (a big circular clay pan) cooking delicious tortillas of yellow corn, my mother would recall her memories, and then, with the captivating voice of a storyteller, she would start her stories in our Jakaltek-Maya language.

Tolob' yet payxa tu'...
hun ni'an kuwis hab' xhq'anni
hunoq bara, maka kab'oq bara manta
haxkam q'ahil hab' yoq no' yalni.

Haktu' hab' xin chu sq'anni no'
hunoq bara maka kab'oq bara manta
yu skolni sb'a no' tet chew.
Yaq ha yet xhq'amb'elax tet no'
tzet ye no'
hakti' hab' chu sta'wi no' lah.

"Mis, mis, k'uxumtoq tx'ow;
tx'ow, tx'ow, holom b'itz'ab';
b'itz'ab' mach xhchanik'oq kaq'e;
kaq'e, kaq'e, ch'iniq'oq asun;
asun, asun, ch'ok yinh sat tz'ayik;
tz'ayik, tz'ayik, xhmak'nitanhoq chew;
chew, chew, xhq'ahnitoq woqan.

In those ancient times...
there was a wild dove who pleaded
for a yard or two of cotton cloth
because, she said, her leg was broken.

She kept on asking and asking
for a yard or two of cotton cloth
to keep her protected from the cold.
But, whenever they asked her
what the problem was
she answered like this:

"Cat, cat, that eats and eats mice;
mice, mice, that gnaw, chewing holes in walls;
walls, walls, that stop the wind;
wind, wind, that carries the clouds;
clouds, clouds, that shadow the sun;
sun, sun, that kills the cold;
and cold, cold, that hurts my leg."

"Ay Jesús, my tortillas are burning!" she would exclaim suddenly, and rush to turn the tortillas on the hot *comal*.

This is how I learned many stories from my mother, especially when there was no access to written materials in the community. Things are changing now and there is less interest in the oral histories and more in written sources such as comics and photonovels. But the elders have continued to tell their stories, utilizing any event in town as an arena for storytelling. Stories are told during communal work projects or during gatherings such as those for petitioning the hand of the bride, marriage, baptism, mourning deaths, house constructions, or reconstruction of the Catholic church. Any communal gathering was used by the elders and storytellers as a forum for stories related to the event. For example, if people were reunited for a death vigil in town, the theme of the stories would be related to life in the underworld — stories of phantoms, spirits and encounters with death. Children would sit on their father's laps. If the storyteller was a man, he would have a male audience; if female, she would have women listening to her. Children, when accompanying their parents, would alternate staying with one or the other, depending on the type of stories being told. I remember following my father when there was a death in town, because men usually sit outside of the house in the darkness and tell scary stories. The women, on the other hand, generally sit inside the house and mourn, sometimes telling stories and anecdotes about the life of the person they are mourning. Storytelling, then, occurs at every opportunity, and the elders usually use those events to instill moral values and open-mindedness in the audience.

Later, when I was a student in a high school in Guatemala, I became more and more aware of and interested in my Mayan heritage. I continued to learn stories from the oral tradition, and because I wanted to keep that heritage alive, I decided to write down some of the stories that my parents had told me or that I had learned from other respected elders in my community.

It is in this way that I collected and reworked these stories that in my childhood were very commonly told by the storytellers. Unfortunately, some of these elders have died and story telling is not as important now because of the constant changes brought to the Mayan communities by the outside world. For this reason, and because of the appreciation and respect that my mother has instilled in me for the memory of my ancestors, I have collected part of this tradition of the Jakaltek-Maya of Guatemala. It is always a difficult task to transform these stories from the oral traditions to the written form, but it is my desire to maintain the creativeness of the Mayan people that is evident in the working and reworking of these stories. Also, it is my desire to leave a testimony to the values of respect, unity and understanding that existed between the

people and their natural and supernatural environment.

For example, in ancient times, birds were considered
the "living colors of the world" and people admired them
profoundly. Among these birds, the buzzard, also called
the "bird who cleans the world," was appreciated because
of its service in cleaning the surroundings of the
villages that lacked toilet or sewage facilities. But,
sadly, when the army arrived in my town in 1982, the
soldiers used buzzards for target practice. Respect for
nature has diminished to the point that modern people
destroy their environment systematically out of
thoughtlessness or selfishness. People can destroy
themselves by not recognizing the value of all living
creatures on earth with whom they should coexist.

These stories, despite their importance as moral
teachings for Mayan children, are also expressions of a
millenarian tradition that has come from the deepest
soul of the Mayan people. Some of the stories in this
volume are very old, and they continue to be passed on
while being reshaped to suit the current historical
situation. Other stories have been created in a more
recent Mayan historical time and have incorporated
western elements in their structure. As in the animal
tales, some stories have included animals such as: the
ox, the donkey, the horse, the chicken, "fierce" dogs,
among others, that were brought to this continent by
the Spaniards. Since then, the Mayan storytellers have
made use of these elements as material available to
them in their collective creations. This creativity can
show us that the present Mayans are also dynamic
actors in the creation, recreation and maintenance of
their own cultural traditions. Mayan communities

16

have been and continue to be active producers of knowledge. Nevertheless, in this effort, the elders have been accused by non-Mayans of carrying on old and absurd ideas that are symbols of their "backwardness." For us Mayans, this is not a symbol of backwardness but a symbol of resistance.

It is only if we are actors in and creators of our own history that we will reaffirm our Mayan ethnic identities within the context of the modern world. In the process, we want all Guatemalan children and the children of the world to learn and understand our history without the distortions and misrepresentations that have been presented until now.

As I present these fables, I am conscious that they are versions of multiple versions, and that the stories told to me by my mother, the elders, and modern Mayan story tellers have also been reworked in the process of transcribing them from the Jakaltek-Maya language to the written form. Some stories did not have a clear ending because the storytellers did not remember them clearly, so I reworked them in consultation with other storytellers.

This small collection of Mayan fables serves moral and literary purposes, but it also represents ethnic conflicts, ecological concerns, communal life and respect for the elders. Some of these animal stories are "trickster's tales" (such as those of the rabbit), others are etiological tales (e.g., how the buzzard got its mission of cleaning the world).

Finally, in presenting these groups of Jakaltek-Maya tales, I hope to illustrate the individual and collective creativity of the contemporary Mayans. Our traditions are alive and vital even though we live in a difficult world of conflicts and violence that tends to sever us more and more from our original traditions. In writing these stories, I am also recognizing the greatness of the Mayan literature. Recounting these tales is like telling the elders and our people that their voices are becoming louder and louder again. Here then, is *The Bird Who Cleans the World and Other Mayan Fables* of the Jakaltek-Maya of Guatemala, Central America.

Victor Montejo
Willimantic, Connecticut 1991

Introduction

Over six million Maya people presently live in Guatemala, southern Mexico and Belize. Since the early 1980's the Maya have begun emigrating to the United States, so that there are now over a hundred thousand Maya living in California, Colorado, Arizona, Florida, and other states. They are part of a civilization over three thousand years old, a civilization whose dramatic and well known classic architecture spanned several hundred years of their history. Victor Montejo is a Jakaltek Maya who is from the Northwestern Highlands of Guatemala near the Mexican Border. In the 1930's anthropologist Oliver La Farge called the Jakaltek Maya "The Year Bearer's People." He was amazed at the Jakaltek skill in remembering and using the complicated ritual calendar of the ancient Maya.

Victor Montejo himself is a bearer of Jakaltek Maya knowledge and wisdom, a perceptive man who brings contemporary Maya experience and thought to life through his work. He is trilingual and tricultural. His first language is Jakaltek Maya, one of the 31 Mayan languages still spoken today in Guatemala, southern Mexico and Belize, and he is likewise fluent in Spanish and English. His own journey through life has taken him from the mountains and corn fields of his community in Guatemala to U.S. life in New York and Connecticut. The trip from his own village to the U.S.

was a bleak odyssey caused by the violence and terror of seeing his own Maya culture destroyed through Guatemalan political violence. That story, published by Curbstone Press in *Testimony: Death of a Guatemalan Village*, is like that of several hundred thousand other Maya who have fled the turmoil of Guatemala for safe haven in Mexico and the U.S.

Victor Montejo transforms this experience into a powerful force for education. He finished his undergraduate degree and is now pursuing his doctorate in anthropology in order to add to the worldwide understanding of the Maya people, bring out new theories and approaches to social science, and bring high quality education to the Maya.

This volume is at once a collection of interesting, sometimes humorous fables that have animal protagonists, and at the same time a window into an indigenous way of thought and experience.

The animal stories from this volume at times remind us of similar stories from the world mythologies. Animals were used in African and Greek stories, such as Aesop's fables to entertain and teach morals. In the U.S., "B'rer rabbit" and Disney cartoons have made animals in fables into loveable children's friends. The animal stories from Maya culture contained here in this book are more substantial than the child-like animals of these other traditions. These Maya animals reveal profound character and personality traits, severe actions, and sometimes unpleasant ideas. People are transformed into vultures and sent in search of rotting carrion and filth to eat. Along with these narratives that include repugnant episodes are others that illustrate Maya irony and humor.

The Trickster, a great figure from many native American mythologies, emerges in this collection in the shape of a deer who steals the horns from the gullible rabbit. Trickster figures are found throughout North and South America and are a major contribution to the world's literature. They are humorous buffoons who make us laugh at their sly antics. They are also powerful beings who transform themselves and the world around them into its present shape. While the deer and the rabbit story explains why deer have horns and rabbits do not, it also points to a world created by activities such as humor, deceit, and naivete. This view of how things came about contrasts sharply with European ideas of evolution proceeding without consciousness or creation, occurring only at the hand of one supreme and serious God.

Maya mythology is considered as "ancient speech," the archaic turns of phrases and old-named characters like these animals who carry only the generic name for their species, such as "Vulture," or "Jaguar." Along with other forms of verbal art, including songs, prayers, declarations, historic legends, and stories, these animal stories make up a coherent repertoire in Maya communities. Some of these stories are taken from the category of talk in Maya that includes "ancient speech." The transformation of two boys into monkeys, for example is found here in this volume as it is in the Quiche Maya epic book of counsel, the *Popol Vuh*. The *Popol Vuh* is rightly considered one of the great books of world literature, and contains sections on the origin of the world, mythological battles, and Maya history up through the conquest. Does the presence of episodes from the *Popol Vuh* suggest that these stories are anecdotes only dimly remembered from the grand plot of the *Popol Vuh*? I do not believe so. It is much more likely that the *Popol Vuh* and grand Maya mythological-historic works like it arose from the anecdotes and episodes told in homes like that of Victor Montejo. Some of these households were fortunate enough to have women such as his mother who saw the value of recounting and retelling these stories and anecdotes about animals and people of other creations over and over again. People like Victor Montejo's mother were more than just the "year bearer's people," they were the shapers of Maya history and cultural theory. In some families these stories were written down, either through glyphic texts or, later, in the Roman alphabet, as in the *Popol Vuh*.

Victor Montejo tells us in his introduction something of the social events of story telling in his home where these fables were first heard. Maya people engage in dialogues for the production of stories, so much so that even the world itself is created out of darkness in the *Popol Vuh* through a dialogue between two gods. To tell a story in Mayan is to engage in conversation, the give and take of questions, comments, shifts in topics, and evaluations of what is said. Montejo describes his home where his mother, the knowledgeable guardian of Maya culture in the family, engages the children in the intellectual game of conversing stories. Some of the stories are told as anecdotes to help make sense of what happens each day, others are told with a clear moral in mind, and still others are told to serve as a catharsis, a humorous safety valve when family conflicts arise. She wove the stories into the lives of Victor and his siblings so well that now, many years later, Victor is compelled to continue the dialogue, now available to us in English. The force of conversational dialogue is also heard in each story. Characters do not so much engage in action as talk to each other. Their schemes, successes, and failures emerge from the talk they have with one another. Description, such as is common in other mythological traditions, is not as important in these Jakaltek Maya stories as conversation.

The time that Victor spent listening to these stories in his home is gone. It has been replaced by years of upheaval, violence, and migration for many people like Victor Montejo. Still, through these dark years, the light of Maya intellectual heritage is still strong. That heritage has been put down on paper and made available to us by a remarkable author. Appreciation is due to Victor Montejo for passing on these fables through this book, a book which is full of Maya illumination.

Allan Burns
University of Florida

THE BIRD WHO
CLEANS THE WORLD

The Bird Who Cleans the World

Our Mayan ancestors spoke of a great flood that covered and destroyed the whole world. They said that the waters rose and rose and rose, flooding the highest mountains and hills and killing everything that lived on the earth. Only one house stood above the flood. In that house all the species of animals entered and hid themselves.

The waters covered the earth for a long time. Then, very slowly, they began to recede, until finally the turbulent waters revealed the earth in its new freedom. When that house was still surrounded by water, they sent forth *Ho ch'ok*, the trumpet bird, to scout the horizon. Since the water was still high the trumpet bird returned quickly, its mission complete.

After a little time more they sent *Usmiq*, the buzzard, to find out how much the water was receding. The messenger, circling through the air, left the house. After a while he flew toward one of the newly uncovered hills and landed with a great hunger.

There he found a large number of dead and rotting animals. Forgetting his mission, he began to devour chunks of the meat until he satisfied his appetite.

When he returned to make his report, the other animals would not let him in among them because his smell was unbearable. And to punish him for his disobedience, *Usmiq* was condemned to eat only dead animals and to clean the world of stench and rottenness.

From that time on the buzzard has been called "The Bird Who Cleans the World" because his duty is to carry off in his beak all that might contaminate the land. *Usmiq*, the buzzard, had to be content with his fate, and thus he went away, forever flying and circling in the air or sitting on the bluffs looking for rotten things to eat.

From Mouse to Bat

When the Creator and Shaper made all the animals, each species was eager to know where they would live, and he assigned their habitats to them.

The happiest were the birds who flew singing to the trees to build their nests. Only Tx'ow, the mouse, didn't move. He stood there open-mouthed contemplating the marvelous flight of the birds.

"Go on," the Creator told him. "Go eat the kernels of corn, seeds, and all the forgotten pieces of food."

But Tx'ow wouldn't move. His body shook with resentment.

The Creator, very angry, picked him up by the tail and threw him in the brush. Tx'ow still could not say a word. He only stared at the flight of the singing birds with his eyes popping out. Then he looked at himself and became very sad. He could make little jumps, but fly? No, he could never achieve that.

Now is the time to act, he said to himself. He decided to call together all the members of his species. There weren't many in those times. Well, he thought, they must be as discontented as I am.

Tx'ow easily convinced his brothers and sisters that they deserved more. One afternoon the delegation of mice came before the god, as he rested from the work of creation.

"What do you want? Speak up," he ordered them.

The delegation tried to speak but it could not. All they could say was, *witz'itz'i, witz'itz'i*.

"What do you want? Speak up," the Creator commanded.

The mice tried with a great effort to speak but they could not.

They only said *witz'itz'i, witz'itz'i*.

The wise god understood what they had come for and he said to them, "You want to fly like the birds?"

The delegation broke out in a big racket of *witz'itz'i, witz'itz'i* nodding their heads yes.

"Very good," the Creator said, "Tomorrow you should appear at *tx'eqwob'al*, the place for jumping, and, I will give you your opportunity."

The mice went away satisfied, believing that a favorable resolution was at hand. To celebrate, there was a great rejoicing among the roots that night.

When the sun came up, the Creator was waiting at the place he had chosen to meet the unhappy mice. "Ready for the test?" he asked. "Those who can jump over this ravine will instantly receive wings and go flying away. And those who do not succeed will remain as they are."

The discontented mice filed up one by one and launched out on the grand adventure. Those whose efforts carried them to the other side received wings and went flying off to the caverns, looking still like mice except for their wings. Those who did not succeed resigned themselves to their fate.

When the great test was over, the Creator warned them, "I don't want you returning to bother me anymore. You who are mice will continue eating grain and seeds. If you want, you can climb the trees and make your nests there. On the other hand those who now have wings will from now on be called *Sotz'*, the bats. For them day will be night. They will feed on mosquitoes and blood, and sleep hanging upside down from the walls of *nhach'en*, the caverns, today and forever."

So it was that *Tx'ow*, the mouse, learned to accept himself and understood that his relatives, the bats, had not found happiness in their new condition either. They lost their tails and their toes grew long in order to cling to the rocks.

The Affair of the Horns

In the beginning, the deer did not have antlers as he has now. Only the rabbit had been favored with such a marvelous means of defense, and the deer coveted those antlers.

One afternoon a deer being chased by dogs arrived in the meadow where the rabbit was browsing. The deer leaped over him in one jump without even noticing.

The rabbit said loudly, "Why are you so much larger than I am? Do you think you have the right to humiliate me?"

"No, friend, I am not humiliating you. I come because I'm eager to admire your fine horns," the deer said.

"Oh, so it's my antlers you like, eh?" the rabbit said proudly.

"Oh, yes. How handsome you are with those horns adorning your head," the deer said.

"The Creator and Shaper gave me these when he made our bodies from the trunks of decayed trees."

"How stingy they were with me that they didn't give me something as valuable as your gift."

"Don't be sorry. They know what they're doing," the rabbit explained.

"Well, maybe I can borrow them for a moment. Wouldn't you like to see how they look on my head?" suggested the deer.

"I can't lend them to you," the rabbit said. "I would feel so small without them."

"I just want to borrow them for a moment, and I'll give them right back. Will you let me?"

"I don't like blockheads and fools, but I'll lend them to you. Just remember, only for a moment."

"Don't worry, friend," the deer assured him.

The rabbit took off his beautiful antlers and carefully placed them on the deer who waited impatiently.

"There, now. Your head is nicely decorated," said the unsuspecting rabbit.

The deer, preening himself, raised his head and asked, "How do I look now, friend rabbit?"

"Magnificent! Your form is brilliant with those branched antlers."

"I'll take a little run and you tell me how they look from a distance." The deer ran a short distance and asked, "How do they look from here?"

"Perfect! You look very elegant with the antlers."

"I'll go a little further and come right back." The deer ran very fast without waiting for the rabbit's consent. The romp which was supposed to be short grew longer and longer and no matter how long the sad rabbit waited, the deer never came back.

He realized that his praise of the deer had worked against him and that he would never recover what he had loaned. With sobs and moans he went off to present himself before the Creator and Shaper, and said, "Oh, Creator, misfortune has fallen on me because of the deer. What will I do now without my antlers? Can they equip me with others to remedy my bad luck? Tell me, tell me, you must solve my problem."

The Shaper approached to listen to the betrayed rabbit's lament and said, "What's so urgent to make you interrupt my sleep?"

"I have come to complain, oh Shaper, of the trickery of the deer. He has cheated me out of my beautiful antlers."

"What did the deer do to rob you of your antlers?"

"I placed them on his head myself because he said he would only borrow them for a moment. That moment passed and now he has not returned, the big liar. He has robbed me shamefully."

"Ah, careless rabbit. What's done is done. Besides I cannot punish the deer for something you did with your own hands. Didn't you know the deer would do anything to have antlers?"

"Now I know I was weak and foolish to let myself be tricked. For that I beg and plead that you give me other antlers, oh Shaper, owner of the parakeets and monkeys, of the foxes and raccoons and of rabbits and deer, please give me more."

The rabbit praised and honored the work of the Creator and Shaper in every way he could, but the only response was this: "You can ask all night and day, but I have no more horns or antlers for you, foolish rabbit. What's more, as punishment, you will live forever without them."

The rabbit felt desperate and continued his fervent pleading, saying, "I hope it isn't so, oh Shaper. I am so small nobody will respect me without antlers. At least if I cannot regain my antlers, make me grow a little."

The incessant begging of the rabbit led the Shaper to reconsider his decision. "Very well, you demanding rabbit. The only thing I can do for you is to draw out your ears and make them long so everyone can see that you are a great animal."

Without saying more the rabbit let the Shaper and Creator stretch his ears upward, and since that time rabbits have had long ears, and learned to be wise and cautious.

How The Serpent Was Born

The care and devotion of a mother for her growing children is enormous. She denies herself and she pours forth the treasure of love from her heart in caring for her child. A mother is an angel. A mother is a treasure. A mother is a special being whom we ought to love every moment of our lives. But many of us do not have hearts big enough to repay her for all that we make her suffer.

There are some who insult and reject their mothers and make them suffer even when they are very old, even though the children ought to bless these women with love and care for all the great pleasures they have given.

So it was that once a certain mother wanted to visit her son's house and rest in the shade of his roof. Since he was her son, he might even give her some tortillas to quiet the great hunger raging in her stomach. But it was not to be so. When the son saw his mother approaching his house, he cursed her and ordered his wife to hide the bubbling pot full of chicken soup that she had cooked for dinner that day. The old lady sat on the doorstep and the son said, "Old woman, why do you come to my house?"

His mother answered, "Son, I only come to rest in the shade of your roof."

"Well, I don't believe I have anything to give you, and besides these visits bore me."

The son and his wife had to work hard to fight the appetites that made them want to devour the succulent chicken soup right in front of the old woman who would then want a share. The old woman grew tired of sitting on the doorstep with not a kind word from her son. She turned back toward her little house, saddened by the ingratitude and indifference of that self-centered and ungrateful son.

"Now the old woman has gone away," the son said to his mate. "Let's eat the chicken soup."

The wife brought out the pot that had been hidden from the old woman's eyes. She put it on the table and lifted off the lid.

"Huuuuuuuyyy, oh Jesús!" she exclaimed.

"What? What's happening?" her husband asked.

The moment she had lifted the lid, instead of the chicken soup she saw a poisonous serpent, coiled in the pot, its head poised, ready to strike. They wanted to kill it, but the snake, shaking its rattles, slithered out to hide.

It is said that the serpent was born this way, the beginning of the bad things that lie waiting for us. It was born of the heart of a son who did not want to know the courage of a mother's saintly love.

The First Monkeys

The first grandmother was walking with her granddaughter and grandson through the forest when they saw a beehive in the hollow of a tree. The grandmother was in a hurry to go home, but the two grandchildren, without asking, climbed the tree and happily began to eat the bees' honey.

The grandmother sat at the foot of the tree to wait for her mischievous grandchildren while they played above, forgetting all about her. The grandmother waited a long time and when the children did not come down, she shouted to them, "Behave yourselves. Come down from that tree right now. I am in a hurry."

"We are eating, grandmother, and our stomachs are still hungry," they answered.

The grandmother continued to wait while the children ate honey and played in the tree. Once again she insisted that the children come down. "Come down, or I will leave you in the tree forever!"

"We are eating, grandmother, and our stomachs are still hungry," they said again.

The children made faces and laughed at their grandmother. By this time they were afraid to come down out of the tree because they had been so disobedient.

The grandmother grew angry and spoke a curse upon them, "My grandchildren, if you do not want to come down from the tree, I will leave you here in the woods forever. Let the honey and the fruits of the trees be your food from now on. Let your faces be changed so that I will not know you."

Saying this, the grandmother took her cane and beat it against the trunk of the tree. She hit the tree trunk four times on each side and in that instant the tree grew so tall and thick that the children, now transformed into monkeys, could not climb down. So they remained there playing among the branches.

Later they hung upside down, watched their grandmother below and laughed, "Hee, hee, heeuuuy!"

The grandmother continued on her way, leaving the monkeys in the tree.

From that time on it is said the curses of a grandmother or a mother can come true at times when children are disobedient.

Sometimes Right Is Repaid with Wrong

The rabbit kept borrowing money and things until he owed half the world. He had not repaid or returned anything. Now he was in a jam and tried to find a way to get out of it.

After some time, he thought of a fantastic idea to escape his worries and his debts, though he would need the hunter to help him out. He went from house to house, visiting all the people from whom he had borrowed money and other things. He told them all that they should come to his house on the following day, and he would return and repay everything he had borrowed.

When the day arrived, the cockroach was the first to request her repayment. The shrewd rabbit put on a worried look and told her, "I know you have come to collect, friend cockroach, and today I will pay you back. But first, please scurry underneath the bed because here comes the hen!"

The cockroach quickly hid herself under the bed, just as the hen entered the room.

"I've come for my things," the hen said. And the rabbit told the hen what he had told the cockroach. "Of course I'll return your things, but first you must hide under the bed because here comes the coyote."

Fearfully, the hen hurried under the bed. But then she spotted the cockroach, snapped it up and swallowed it in a flash.

"I want the money you owe me," the coyote announced.

The clever rabbit replied, "I will certainly repay you, but quick, hide under the bed because here comes the jaguar."

The coyote, trembling at the mention of the jaguar, quickly leaped under the bed where he found the hen and hungrily ate her.

"I've come to collect what you owe me," growled the jaguar menacingly.

The rabbit remained nonchalant and responded, "I'm going to repay you, I promise. But first please hide under my bed because here comes the hunter!

The jaguar, fearing the hunter, squeezed under the bed in a flash. There he found himself next to the coyote and treated himself to a feast.

The hunter came running into the room with his rifle ready and called to the rabbit, "Here I am. Where is that troublesome jaguar you complained about?"

The rabbit pointed under the bed. In this way he repaid all his brothers who had once offered help in a time of need.

The Disobedient Child

In old times in *Xaqla'* Jacaltenango there was a
very disobedient child who often disappointed his
parents. No matter how hard they tried to teach him,
he never changed.

One afternoon the boy ran away from home looking
for someone who would tolerate his mischief. Walking
through the woods he discovered a lonely little house
and ran up to it. On the porch of the straw-covered
house sat an old man, smoking peacefully. The boy stood
before him without saying hello or any other word of
greeting.

When the old man noticed the boy's presence, he
stopped smoking and asked him, "Where do you want to
go, boy?"

"I am looking for someone who can give me
something to eat," the boy answered.

The wise old man, who already knew the boy's story,
said, "No one will love you if you continue being so bad."

The boy did not respond except to laugh.

Then the old man smiled and said, "You can stay
with me. We will eat together."

The boy accepted his offer and stayed in the old
man's house. On the following day before going to work,
the old man told the boy: "You should stay in the house,
and the only duty you will have is to put the beans to

cook during the afternoon. But listen well. You should only throw thirteen beans in the pot and no more. Do you understand?"

The boy nodded that he understood the directions very well. Later when the time arrived to cook the beans, the boy put the clay pot on the fire and threw in thirteen beans as he had been directed. But once he had done that he began to think that thirteen beans weren't very many for such a big pot. So, disobeying his orders, he threw in several more little fistfulls.

When the beans began to boil over the fire, the pot started to fill up, and it filled up until it overflowed. Very surprised, the boy quickly took an empty pot and divided the beans between the two pots. But the beans overflowed the new pot, too. Beans were pouring out of both pots.

When the old man returned home he found piles of beans, and the two clay pots lay broken on the floor.

"Why did you disobey my orders and cook more than I told you to?" the old man asked angrily.

The boy hung his head and said nothing. The old man then gave him instructions for the the next day. "Tomorrow you will again cook the beans as I have told you. What's more I forbid you to open that little door over there. Do you understand?"

The boy indicated that he understood very well.

The next day the old man left the house after warning the boy to take care to do exactly what he had been told. During the afternoon the boy put the beans on the fire to cook. Then he was filled with curiosity. What was behind the little door he had been forbidden to open?

Without any fear, the boy opened the door and discovered in the room three enormous covered water jars. Then he found three capes inside a large trunk. There was one green cape, one yellow cape and one red cape. Not satisfied with these discoveries, the boy took the top off the first water jar to see what it contained.

Immediately the water jar began to emit great clouds that quickly hid the sky. Frightened and shivering with cold, the boy opened the trunk and put on the red cape. At that instant a clap of thunder exploded in the house. The boy was turned into thunder and lifted to the sky where he unleashed a great storm.

When the old man heard the thunder he guessed that something extraordinary had happened at home, and he hurried in that direction. There he discovered that the forbidden door was open and the top was off the jar of clouds from which churning mists still rose toward the sky. The old man covered the jar and then approached the trunk with the capes. The red cape, the cape of storms, was missing. Quickly the old man put on the green cape and regained control over the sky, calming the great storm. Little by little the storm subsided, and soon the man returned to the house carrying the unconscious boy in his arms.

A little while later the old man uncapped the same jar and the clouds which had blackened the sky returned to their resting place, leaving the heavens bright and blue again. When he had done this the old man capped the jar again and put away the red and green capes.

Through all of this the boy remained stunned and soaked with the rains until the kind old man restored his spirit and brought him back to normal. When the boy was alert again and his fear had left, the old man said, "Your disobedience has almost killed you. You were lucky that I heard the storm and came to help.

Otherwise you would have been lost forever among the clouds."

The boy was quiet and the old man continued.

"I am Qich Mam, the first father of all people and founder of Xaqla', he who controls the rain and waters the community's fields when they are dry. Understand, then, that I wish you no harm and I forgive what you have done. Promise me that in the future you will not disobey your parents.

The boy smiled happily and answered, "I promise, Qich Mam, I promise." Qich Mam patted him gently and said, "Then return to your home and be useful to your parents and to your people."

From that time on the boy behaved differently. He was very grateful for the kindness of the old man who held the secret of the clouds, the rains, the wind and the storms in his hands.

The Tail of The Dog

Of the origins of the world only the dog could speak. He went around everywhere, revealing the secret of the creation of things and the origin of god.

When the great god realized the talkative dog could not hold his tongue and keep the secrets, the Creator decided: "Let this talker's marvelous tongue be taken from his head and put it behind him, and let what is now behind him, be attached to his head.

So it is now that when the dog wants to speak and tell things, no expression appears on its face but there it is behind him, the tail that came from his head.

And so the dog has stayed with us, he who once betrayed his secrets. And even now, he only moves his tail when he wants to tell us something or when he is happy with his master.

The Toad and The Buzzard

Once upon a time at the end of the rainy season, a tired buzzard landed on a meadow where an enormous toad happened to be wandering about looking for friendship. With long and steady leaps, the toad approached with a big smile to greet the new arrival.

"Hello, good friend, the toad said cordially.

"Hello, how goes it," the buzzard answered.

Because of the confidence the buzzard inspired in him, the toad did not hesitate to explain his desire. "As you see, Señor Buzzard, I am walking about looking for friends. Would you like to be my best friend?"

"Certainly I would," the buzzard answered without beating around the bush.

The toad leaped several times with joy since he had already looked everywhere without finding a friend of any kind. And here he had found not only a friend, but a friend with wings. How interesting.

Upon seeing the toad jump so happily, the buzzard wanted to prove his friendship. "Friend toad," he said, "I will give you a free ride through the air so you may know strange places — children, flowers, forests, rivers, lakes, and seas."

Upon hearing this, the enormous toad could not contain his joy.

"When will we go, friend buzzard?" he asked impatiently.

"This very day if you like," the buzzard replied.

"Let's not lose any more time then, friend. Carry me through the air, quick, quick," the toad insisted.

"Calm down, friend. First I must look for something to fill my empty stomach. That's why I stopped here."

The buzzard picked through many things lying on the ground until finally he found a juicy meal of the kind he liked.

"Hurry up, friend buzzard, I'm dying to go," the toad shouted.

The buzzard came up and said, "Climb on my wings and we will fly."

The toad climbed up quickly, and the buzzard rose in his majestic flight. As they flew the toad opened his big eyes wider and wider to see the marvels that had remained hidden from him for so long. They made two or three turns over each place, flying ever farther from the meadow. Suddenly the buzzard burped and the gas almost suffocated the toad. Unable to ignore the stink, the toad shouted rudely, "Ooof, how your beak smells!"

The buzzard turned his head to his friend and answered, "What are you saying, friend toad?"

"I said that it is beautiful to fly through the air."

The buzzard continued flapping his wings and flying over the clouds. After a while the toad began to complain again about the stink from his friend's beak. "Chish! the stench of your beak makes me sick, cruddy buzzard."

The buzzard had heard him the first time, but paid no attention to the toad's words. But when the toad repeated his rude comments, the buzzard was gravely insulted. He wanted to respond immediately, but decided to pretend he had not understood. Quite pleasantly he asked, "What are you trying to say, friend toad?"

The toad, trying to pretend, stuttered, "s-s-s-saying that I feel very happy flying with you."

The buzzard continued flying, hoping that the friend he carried would mend his ways and recognize him for the friend he was. But the stupid toad continued being rude and insulting to his kind friend. Once more the smell washed over the toad and he exclaimed, "Oooof! the stench of your body and your beak offends me, dirty bird."

The buzzard stopped flapping his wings, and without asking the toad what he had said, the buzzard said, "Very well, my friend. We have gotten to know each other and you insist on rejecting me because of what I am. What would happen in the future if we remained friends? Good-bye, ungrateful toad," the buzzard said and rose straight up toward the clouds.

As he flew the toad lost his grip and who knows where the remains of this ingrate fell, this toad who did not know how to speak with a sincere friend?

The Toad And The Crab

The toad was resting in the cool spring when suddenly a crab arrived to enjoy the same pleasures. The toad, who often played jokes on others, said to the crab, "Where are you going with your oars?" He was, of course, making fun of the crab's long pincers and legs.

The crab answered with his own joke. "It seems I've arrived in the city of Big Mouth."

"Big mouth, but a good singer," responded the toad who knew the crab was making fun of his large mouth.

"Delight me with your music, then," the crab commanded.

"Very well," said the toad, and swallowing enough air to puff himself up, he began like this:

> May you, may I
> may I, may you,
> may you, may I
> may I....

The crab backed away, leaving behind the hoarse toad who continued his croaking song and its monotonous verses.

The Proof Of The Mice

Long ago a husband and wife with evil in their hearts lived in the house of a generous man. The owner of the house treated them kindly as if they were his own children, and he helped them with their needs when they asked. Thus, they lacked nothing nor did they have too much.

As the days passed something began to disturb the owner. From time to time some valuable thing would disappear from the house, and he could not tell who had taken it. "I can't believe that those who live with me would do this. I have loved them as my own children, but to dispel my doubts, I will put them to a test today." So he quietly and carefully found two big mice and hid them in a basket on the table.

Then he said to the man and wife as he always did, "Please watch over the house, especially the basket which contains very valuable things. Don't touch it. I will return in a little while."

The old man left the house thinking, if they respect my things, they will obey my warning, but if they are the ones who have robbed me, they will not hesitate to look in the basket.

So it was. As soon as the old man left the house, the husband and wife were curious to see the valuables in the basket. As they lifted the top, the two mice escaped at breakneck speed. The husband, who realized that this was a test, went all over, even up on the roof, looking for the mice. It was no use.

He was still looking when the old man returned home. Upon seeing the empty basket he became so angry that he asked his guests to leave immediately. "Get out of my house, you ingrates! I have given you everything, and you haven't even been able to respect my property or be honest and fair. What could I expect from you if you were to stay with me longer?"

The husband and wife left the house in shame and with a very bad reputation as the old man shouted after them the popular refrain: "No one is well received who has learned how to steal."

I know the old man was right
to drive them from his angry sight.
Hadn't he found out the vice
of those he cast into the night?
His proof, the disappearing mice.

Laziness
Should Not Rule Us

Three jaguars were dying of hunger, but they didn't want to go out into the forest to look for food. Just then Rabbit came upon them and asked with great concern, "Why are you complaining so, my friends?"

"Well, we are dying for something to eat," answered the jaguars.

"What of these great claws and fangs? What are they for if not to catch your food?"

"Yes," the jaguars said, "But we would have to go out and look for it."

"Well, then," Rabbit said, "you need someone to carry you out into the forest. Very good. I can carry all of you. Climb into this net."

So they quickly climbed into his net.

When they were in and the net was tied shut, Rabbit found a long green *guava* stick. With the stick he beat the jaguars. "Take this! This is what you deserve," he shouted. "You are built like great hunters, but you don't want to exert yourselves." He whacked them hard again. "This is what you deserve, you lazy beasts."

Rabbit left them lying there. The jaguars learned from that beating that laziness is the origin of much misfortune.

Advice From A Jackass

A peasant from the warm lands was ploughing his field in the full heat of the day with a tired and sweating ox who did not want to finish the work.

Passing near a jackass who was quietly grazing, the ox stopped and planted his feet with unusual stubbornness. The jackass took advantage of the moment to tell his comrade, "Don't work any longer. Fall down as if you are sick, or kick this executioner who drives you."

"Good idea," said the ox and threw himself to the ground.

The peasant had no means to lift him. He twisted his tail and beat him like a drum but nothing got him up. Tired of working over the insolent animal he straightened up and shouted furiously, "Bring me the jackass. The jackass will finish the work."

Other peasants untied the jackass from his post and hitched him to the harness and plough. Under the harsh whip he began to plough instead of the ox who now found himself in the jackass's place, grazing in the delicious shade.

The jackass snorted furiously and began to kick high in the air as was his nature, but each time he was so imprudent the blows of the whip fell more strongly.

All this happened while the ox peacefully chewed his cud, observing from a distance his friend who had given him such magnificent advice.

On the other hand the donkey sweated and sweated under a rain of whip blows and insults, cursing the unfortunate moment in which he had given a jackass's advice.

Who Cuts the Trees
Cuts His Own Life

When I was a small boy my father used to tell me, "Son, don't cut the little green trees whenever you please. When you do that you are cutting short your own life and you will die slowly."

This warning always worried me, especially since at times I have carelessly cut some little tree by the side of the road with my machete.

My father's warning was nothing new, but something the old ones have said since distant times. And my father who knew their teachings, repeated it to me and my brothers. Now when I hear about pollution, erosion, and deforestation, I realize the value of the old philosophy. These things are signs of the slow death that our elders have always foreseen when they said, "Who cuts the trees as he pleases, cuts short his own life."

The Ungrateful Alligator

It is said that in the days of the terrible drought even the fountains dried up. The fish and the frogs in the drying springs could not move quickly enough to the distant creeks, rivers, or lakes and they died.

A boy passing by saw an alligator languishing, fighting for breath, and without thinking twice, he carried the alligator to the deep pool of a nearby river where it happily remained.

Some time later, the boy wanted to swim, and he waded into the same pool where he had once put the alligator. The ungrateful alligator appeared and wanted to devour his servant. "I'll eat you, my friend. I'll eat you today because I'm hungry. How much I'd like to try such a sweet, tasty morsel to satisfy my appetite."

Very much frightened, the boy answered, "Mister Alligator, please be quiet. Don't you realize who I am? I'm the one who saved you from the drought! I ask you to please let me go. You might like to repay the favor that I did so nicely for you one day."

"I know nothing of what you are saying, nor do I recognize past favors. The only thing I know is that I'm hungry and I'm going to eat you up right now."

A rabbit, who had been watching from nearby, heard them arguing. To put an end to this matter he called for the dog, the horse, and the deer so they could speak of man and show their appreciation.

Those he summoned gladly appeared. "As for me," said the dog, "they force me to follow the tracks of the deer. Little difference it makes to cursed men if I have to run through thorns and thistles. And when I give them their succulent supper, all that they throw me are bones. What will happen when I am old? Surely they'll call me a fool, and they'll give me nothing, not even bones. So I say that man is evil and I swear it by the darling of my eyes."

"Now let me speak," said the deer, stretching his long neck. "Of course the dog pursues me on orders from ungrateful man who looks at us hungrily and sees only the finest meat for his plate. I keep my head high, ears cocked, always ready to flee danger. It is man who brings all my trouble, my sleeplessness, my fear."

"And I," said the tranquil horse, "Yes, he beats me with his stick. He never asks if I am sick or if I can bear the burden he loads on me. And worse, what I fear even more, is when he mounts me without caring and pulls the bit in my mouth. Ay! If I don't gallop just as he pleases, he's full of foul insults."

"And is it possible Mister Alligator, that this boy could have carried you all the way to this pool as I have heard?" said the rabbit.

"Well, yes. It's true. When the stream where I lived disappeared in the drought, I believe he carried me in a net."

"Oh, words will not convince me, only the facts themselves. Will you put yourself in the net to see if it's really true that this boy can carry you?"

"Why not. Look here, I'm in. Let the boy come lift me and so, Rabbit, you will believe it. Then I'll devour the boy."

The alligator let himself be closed inside the boy's limp net. Thus at the rabbit's insistence, since he was known for his good advice, the boy carried the reptile all the way back to the dry stream and he left him there with his ingratitude.

The Little Boy
Who Talked With Birds

The song of the birds is a salute to life and in each song is a message of love.

Happy are they who can understand the notes trilled so clearly by the beautiful birds.

* * *

Some say that birds speak with each other in their own language and that this language is universal and full of harmonies that have no equal in the world. Among the Mayans who lived long ago there were people who could understand clearly those messages of the birds and who enjoyed immensely those beautiful dialogues and all the words they sang. Sometimes they were quick to heed the prophecies they heard. Sometimes the birds only sang, but other times their notes were messages for passers-by.

So it was with the young worker who went with his father to work in the fields every day. He never complained, even when his father treated him badly. On the contrary, he loved and respected his parents like any decent boy. When lunchtime came, the father and his son would sit in the shade of a tree beside the fields and drink the grain soup and eat their *tortillas* with beans and the wild *chipilín* greens. At this hour a beautiful bird also arrived and perched in the tree above them. Each day he sang in the same way.

After listening intently to the bird's song, the boy would laugh, or sometimes only smile so his father would not notice his odd behavior. This happened every day he went to work in the cornfield. Whenever the bird began to sing, the boy would laugh, trying not to annoy his father.

One day, however, the father asked gruffly, "What is it saying, this bird that comes to sing to us?"

"It just feels like singing," the boy answered.

"And why do you laugh when it sings if it is only singing?"

"Only because I enjoy hearing it sing, nothing more," the boy said.

"If it pleases you, then it is because it is saying something. Tell me!" the angry father ordered.

"It doesn't say anything," the boy replied casually.

"Don't try to hide it from me. Tell me quickly or I'll give you a beating!" the father warned.

The father's threats grew more severe. Because the boy did not want to anger his father anymore, he said, "Since you insist, I will tell you. It says you will have to salute me one day."

The father felt insulted. "Salute you! Are you crazy?"

"No. It is not I who says it, but the bird."

The father became even angrier and exclaimed, "All right, how is it going to happen that a father salutes a son?"

"I don't know. You insisted and I have only told you what the bird was singing."

The father was very upset by all of this because he thought his son was losing respect for him and that a day would come when the boy would humiliate him. The rigid man began to treat the boy even more unjustly, finally throwing him out of the house.

The boy bore this injustice patiently and wandered aimlessly about the world, like an orphan or a lost child. When he had travelled for a long time, the boy came to the domain of a great chief where by chance he heard the following proclamation:

He who can interpret the squawks of the crows who come every afternoon fluttering about the chief's window, can marry the chief's daughter and inherit the kingdom.

Many had tried to pass the test, but their interpretations had not satisfied the chief. The proof of this was that the crows kept coming to the window every afternoon to disturb the chief, never heeding any reply to their squawking. Then someone told the chief that a strange boy had arrived in the community, and the chief immediately ordered that he be brought before him.

The boy came before the great chief and asked why he had been called. The chief replied, "Two crows come here every afternoon to flutter about and squawk through my window. Now I am fed up with them. How should I know what they want? Many have tried to understand what these birds say, but they have all failed. Stay here until they come and let's see if you can resolve this problem."

That afternoon the two birds arrived at the usual hour and began to squawk loudly. The boy approached the window and then smiled as he listened to the excited squawking. When they finished, the boy told the chief what he had understood.

"The male crow says that the female crow abandoned her eggs and that he had to keep them warm until the little boy crow and little girl crow hatched. And the female crow says the male crow didn't carry any food to the nest and that's why she disappeared. But now she has reappeared to claim her legitimate children, the two baby crows."

"Ay, *caramba*, and now, now what do we do?" the chief asked.

The boy answered quickly. "Well, the male crow should take the little girl crow and female should take the little boy crow."

So the boy told this to the crows that very afternoon and they were immediately satisfied with the solution, and flew off happily.

After that, the chief was satisfied, and he soon fulfilled his vow by marrying his daughter to the boy, who soon inherited all that he owned. All the people from the neighboring villages attended the wedding feast. Among them came two old people whom the boy soon recognized.

Everyone came forward to salute the new chief, including the old couple. They greeted him respectfully, "Good health to you, great lord!" the trembling old man said.

The young chief rushed forward to greet the old man and said, "Don't bow before me and don't salute me, because I am your son. Don't you remember me and that bird and how you made me tell you what he said in his song?"

"Oh, my son! Forgive me for what I have done to you," the old man sobbed.

The boy embraced his parents and announced, "Don't worry, father. I'm not angry. From today on, you and mother will live near me so our family can be reborn in peace and happiness."

And so, when the prophecy of the bird who sang by the cornfield came to pass, thus ended the story of the boy who understood the language of the birds.

The Child Who Saw Visions

The old dog Tusik went out into the yard every night and barked tirelessly. His big ears stood up and leaned forward as if he spied on the far horizon devilish ghosts and visions about to throw themselves on him. This scrawny dog pawed lazily at his fleas, and at night he barked fervently and ceaselessly at the distance. This habit allowed neither the owners of the house nor the neglected dog himself any peace.

Mothers said to their children, "Dogs who howl all night like Tusik have visions and can see strange things that other dogs cannot see, much less us humans. And far from being good luck for the dog, it becomes a misfortune that keeps him from sleeping. And what's worse, he is always terrified."

The little boy Tik-Lol, who heard this, wanted to see if it was true. One afternoon, ignoring his mother's words, he grabbed the dog and wiped from its open eyes the thick green ooze that gathered in the corners. Then he rubbed his own eyes with it as if it were an ointment that he had taken from Tusik's runny eyes.

A short time later the boy began to see strange things, and his alarmed cries woke up the neighbors at night. "Aaayy, what's that! Don't let it catch me! Uuuuyyy!"

Every night his cries joined the howling of the dog who stared trembling at the horizon. The little Tik-Lol could not bear up under this evil. He became horribly thin and finally he ceased to exist.

From that time it was clear that no one should rub his eyes with the phlegm from the eyes of dogs who see visions at night, or what happened when Tik-Lol disobeyed his parents might happen to them.

The Snail and the Minnow

A lordly snail. forgetting his limitations, challenged a bold minnow to a race.

"Very good," the minnow replied. "We will run the course you want, but the race must have its rules and a prize for the winner."

"I will put up my sombrero!" the snail said without thinking and having nothing else to offer. And so they made their deal.

The minnow swam round and round in the river while the snail tried his best to start the race. What happened then? Well, just what had to happen. The lordly snail lost his sombrero!

The Curious Mice

Two country mice sat on a roof looking through a neighbor's bedroom window just as a child was about to be born. They seemed upset and didn't chat so much as argue. "Will it be a boy child? Or a girl child?" So they wondered, more worried than the people below who waited to deliver the child.

One mouse said, "Oh, women. Bang, they cover the pot, they hide everything, even the onions. So if this baby's a woman, we're lost. Now men, men are more careless. They hide nothing and we have our mouths full. If this is a boy, a man...*witz'itz'i, witz'itz'i!* we will be singing!

"Oh no," the other said. Sure it's the men who plant the grain, but they also lay out the traps. And if by bad luck we fall into their hands, it's adiós seeds, adiós cakes, adiós grain! Now, women, they are even afraid of us, and we can pass through their kitchens. So if this is a girl, all very good, it's *witz'itz'i! witz'itz'i!* we'll be singing."

So the two mice weighed their views of man and of woman. And while they fell into deep debate comparing their viewpoints, a hungry cat came prowling and meeowing, putting to flight the two rodents.

No one knows what they concluded since they fled, as always, into their cave. If someone had given them the good news, it would be *witz'itz'i*, *witz'itz'i*, so they would sing because the origin and object of the argument that set them apart and kept them awake was a boy and a girl, born that night as twins.

The Work of the Mosquito

The mosquito goes about his work always at grave risk, never knowing if he will come home alive. Most often he dies as he is piercing his victim. Poor fellow, when luck runs out. He's surprised in the act and a slap of the victim's palm leaves him flattened where he worked. If he is agile and fortunate enough, then he satisfies his appetite and goes buzzing away.

So it was that a mosquito buzzed off happily after stabbing an old man who was sleeping. On the road he met another mosquito who was still looking for a meal, and he asked him:

"Where are you going, brother mosquito?"
"I'm going to drink some blood in the dell."
"And when will you come back again?"
"Only the stroke of the hand will tell."

The War of the Wasps

One day a cricket, wanting to rest for the night, arrived in the jaguar's cave. Without the consent or even the knowledge of the mansion's owners, he climbed into a little crevice. From there, as is the custom or the vice of his kind, he began to chirp in the middle of the night, disturbing the holy peace and irritating the big family of carnivores.

The chirping of the cricket infuriated the residents of the cave and was heard for a great distance, tearing the silence of the night and disturbing their sleep. After several hours had passed the jaguars (*b'alam*) could bear the scandalous chirping no more. They got up with the clear intention of exterminating the source of that disagreeable music.

They clawed at the walls on all sides of the caves looking for the source of their misery, but the night was too dark, and the cricket had hidden himself in the highest and darkest crevice.

When dawn came, the jaguars got up in a bad mood and watched for the unknown visitor who had kept them up all night. The cricket took one hop and revealed himself. The jaguars were very puzzled to see how small a musician had annoyed them so much.

"Come down from there," they demanded.

The cricket remained where he was near his hiding place. If he came down, he surely would never again serenade the peaceful night. So, fearing the great danger below, he did not move.

The jaguars insisted again. "Come down and take what you deserve."

Then the cricket quickly looked for some safe way to escape. He said very seriously, "What a shame! You who are called 'Kings of the Animals', want to do away with a simple and defenseless evening troubadour who only wants to celebrate love in his songs. You do not deserve your noble title."

The jaguars felt insulted and replied, "Then call whomever you want to help you, because you are not going to humiliate us before anything or anybody.

The cricket answered, "If I call other insects to defend me, I am sure that we will triumph. But my wish is that there be peace and tranquility among us all."

"How can some simple insects conquer us, we who are the strongest of the animals?" roared the jaguars. "Eah! Let them all come to defend you, and we'll wait here among our own kind with claws and fangs."

A rabbit who was listening to the discussion set out to help the cricket. Quickly he went through the forest carrying large hollow gourds, looking for all kinds of wasps. The wasps all agreed to help the cricket. So with all the venom stored in their stingers, they climbed into the gourds to be carried to where the event would take place.

The jaguars, too, were calling other animals to their side. They gathered the largest and most ferocious, like the pumas, the mountain cats, and the wild boars. They all gathered on the grassy plain where the cricket approached them to say that everyone was ready. The jaguars, hearing that their opponents were ready, threw themselves forward furiously, roaring and causing a great panic among the other inhabitants of the forest.

The rabbit waited for an opportune moment. When he thought the time was right, he uncovered the big gourds and let loose a torrent of furious wasps who went after the bodies of their enemies, where they buried their stingers.

The ferocious beasts were covered with stinging wasps, and no matter how much they roared, ran and shook themselves, they couldn't get rid of their attackers. Each time, the wasps stung more furiously, injecting their poison in the eyes, the noses, the tails, and everywhere, tormenting the jaguars horribly. Tired of fighting in vain, the jaguars rolled on the ground trying to free themselves of their tireless persecutors.

It is hard to believe, but so it was that the cricket, with help from the rabbit and the wasps, succeeded in conquering so easily the fearsome jaguars who ran away in all directions seeking refuge and salvation in their caves and under the bushes.

The King of the Animals

The jaguar (B'alam) and the mountain lion (Kaq-koh) sent a declaration throughout the jungle. "Let all the animals come together, from the greatest to the smallest without exception, to elect the king of the animals." The citizens faced a delicate decision — to elect their delegates proudly. All the citizens of the jungle had arrived from even the most secret places. Shouting and cheering, they supported their favorite. The animals came from everywhere to debate the merits of the contenders. The jungle shook with the clamor.

The lion remained calm. The jaguar, however, was pacing nervously, even wildly, among the crowds, assuring himself that everyone was present. Suddenly he said, "One is missing, the rabbit!"

So it was. The rabbit was the only animal who had not come at the appointed time.

"The election is a tie and we need the rabbit to decide," said the jaguar. "I'll go get him whether it's for better or for worse."

This jaguar wanted to win by any means. He didn't take long to find the rabbit who was sleeping beneath some green fronds. Very diplomatically he asked:

"What's up, my fine friend? You haven't come to the election. After all, you are he who performs great deeds and makes great decisions. Now you are absent when we need you most."

"Oh, I'm very sorry, Señor Jaguar. I am very sick and I can't get up from my cot. Perhaps you would like to carry me on your back." The clever rabbit looked very sick and held a wad of bean leaves to his head.

"Climb on my back and we will be off, since everyone is waiting for us." The jaguar loaded the sick-looking rabbit on his back and soon they arrived at the field where the election was to be decided.

"The rabbit has arrived! The wise rabbit has arrived," everyone shouted at once. The jaguar stepped to one side twitching his enormous tail while he awaited the decisive vote from the rabbit.

The rabbit was quick to speak up. "One moment, friends. Before we arrive at such an important decision, it is wise to get to know the candidates more thoroughly. So let's see. The jaguar seems a good candidate because he is so agile, and with such claws he is a good hunter. But for this very reason he is a serious danger to all of us. As king he would have complete liberty to exterminate us in order to satisfy his ever voracious appetite. Now the lion is a little more peaceful and less impulsive than the jaguar. For this reason I vote for the lion as our king!"

All the other animals seconded the rabbit's wise decision. And so the mountain lion was confirmed the king of the jungle. The jaguar went away defeated. He had learned that the person who has his ideals and principles well-guarded cannot be easily corrupted, even if you carry him a long way.

The Loudmouth and Death

A loudmouth began talking about death, praising its quality in no uncertain terms.

"I admire my friend Death who never plays favorites. For her there are no differences, not color nor race nor dress. She touches everyone, the nobodies and the bigwigs. She never plays favorites by age. Child, youth and elder are equal. I admire that with all my heart and invite death to be my good friend."

Death quickly answered his invitation and soon they became friends. Time passed without worry and with many joys. Then Death returned, looking intently and anxiously for her fine companion. And he, upon seeing her, almost fainted.

"Compadre, I've come to take you with me off to the place you have earned. So quick, let's go, like a good friend. Let me tell you, there's nothing to fear."

"No, dear woman! don't touch me! Don't you remember we promised to be friends, the very best friends?"

"Ha, ha ha! What are you saying, compadre? Some time ago didn't you go and declare I was a friend of great honor and virtue?"

"Yes, but...Well, I'm just not ready. I've got a lot of projects going, and besides, we are very good friends!"

"Well, today you're going with me in spite of the unfinished projects. Don't you see, I have no favorites and look on everyone as equal? What do friendships mean to me — or race, clothes, color or language?"

The loudmouth was taken, leaving everything behind, unfinished, just as it was.

The Hen and the Frog

One day the frog was in her pond jealously watching over her eggs when along came the hen looking for a place to nest. After a moment of silence the hen laid a large egg. Feeling happy and proud, she began to cackle, shattering the peace the frog was enjoying at the edge of the pond.

Irritated by this noise, the frog jumped up onto the shore to interrupt the cackling. "Quiet, quiet, Madame Pompador! I'd like to know what all this fuss is about."

"Well, I've laid an egg, a magnificent egg. A big, handsome, new egg." With this the hen reached under herself with her beak and rolled out the egg. The frog mocked her. "Well, well, well, just one egg, and you make such a racket. What would you do if you had laid the countless eggs I have? Look at these long strings of eggs. And I am not going around boasting and praising myself."

"Well, so it is, my dear friend," said the chicken. "But the eggs I lay serve as the farmer's food. Yours, so far as I know, though they are counted by hundreds or thousands, don't have as much essential use as one of mine."

PLUK! the embarrassed frog disappeared under the water. Although she heard the hen cackling over other eggs, she didn't come out to make comparisons. She learned from her rash conduct that quality and not quantity determines the value of a product.

The Man and the Buzzard

A man who had fine lands to plant didn't much like to work. His wife suffered deprivation until almost everything in the house disappeared. The man, instead of going to work, just sat around, passing the day producing nothing.

One of those days he saw a buzzard circling in the sky, lazily flapping his wings without a care in the world. "Oh, how I'd like to be that bird!" the man said, stretched out having a siesta as always.

The buzzard came down and sat near the man. The man came near and said with great interest, "I love to see you fly, good friend. I can see very well that you have the freedom to fly wherever you like. Ah, if only I too had wings. I would fly all over the world and no one would oblige me to work as they do now. What do you say we trade places. You stay here in my place and I take your wings and fly?"

The buzzard answered, "Mister, at least you have land to work. And what would your wife say if we changed places?"

"I don't care. I prefer to enjoy myself and fly around without working rather than remain a bored prisoner here."

The buzzard said, "The life of a buzzard isn't very pleasant, either. Sometimes we find nothing to eat and we must bear the hunger. Now you, you can eat at whatever hour you want if only you work to grow what you need."

"It may be so, but I would still like to trade," insisted the man.

"What if you change your mind after the trade? I think you'd be better off cultivating your land and taking care of your wife."

The man insisted again, more strongly. "No, I want nothing more than to trade places. Do this favor right away. I want to be a buzzard."

It is said that the buzzard then gave in.

"What you ask for I will give you. Lie down on the ground and I will step over you three times." He did so.

The "buzzard" stretched his wings and went flying off.

The "man," identical to the one who had disappeared, went on his way home.

When the man reached the house the woman did not detect the change, but she did smell a certain bad odor.

"What have you been eating that makes you smell so putrid?" she shouted at him.

"It is because I was sweating and the smell of weeds clings to my body," the man said.

Because the woman insisted, the man bathed himself and little by little the odor began to disappear.

After a while the woman began to feel very happy about her companion's changed and repentant conduct. The man had begun to work very hard, and they always had enough to eat in the house. So she too got up at dawn to make the meal which he would take to work with him.

On the other hand the "buzzard" went flying aimlessly about. When he felt hungry he came to earth to try what the other buzzards were eating. The other buzzards sensed something strange about him and pecked at him mercilessly. Then he would withdraw and fly around, hungry, looking for another meal. The same thing always happened. He could never find a place among the other buzzards.

Some time later the buzzard arrived at the place where he had first made the trade. And when by chance he met the man who used to be a buzzard, he jumped up and presented himself, begging. "Forgive me if I bother you, but I want your help in changing my appearance. I want to return to my position as a man. As a buzzard I am almost dying of hunger. The other buzzards won't let me eat, and when I do get a bite, I throw up even those things that buzzards like so much."

"I am very sorry friend, but I can no longer oblige you. What is done, is done. I begged you not to make the trade."

"I know that I was stubborn, but now I repent my foolishness. Let's change again. I beg you."

"I've already told you it is impossible. Besides I am tending very good crops, and your wife is very happy with me because I have treated her well."

The buzzard shook his wings, pleading. "Have pity on my misfortune. Wherever I go the other buzzards reject me. How can I live like this? Please, have compassion!"

The man answered, "I advised you earlier that the life of a buzzard is not as happy as some people think. We all have to work to get our daily meal."

"Yes, now I understand," the buzzard said. "Before I only wanted to fly and fly, looking around the world without worrying about my home, my land, and my people. But now I have returned. I want to stay in this little corner of the world."

Upon hearing the buzzard's sincerity, the man agreed. "Well, all right. We will trade again. But do you promise to work and to take care of your wife as I've taken care of her?"

"That is what I'll do. I promise."

"All right, we will trade, because in the end you are really made as a man and I as a buzzard. I do not want to keep what is yours. Lie down again and I will step over you just as I did when you first asked to trade places."

So it was that the man stepped over the buzzard three times, and in a wink the two had changed again. The buzzard became a man, and the real buzzard went flying away through the air, flapping his wings happily and looking for his own world where other buzzards fly and make circles in the air, far from the problems of men.

When the man arrived at home, the wife was surprised to see a different husband. He had gone off to work robust and chubby and after a few hours he had returned skinny and boney.

"What happened that you've come back so thin?" she asked.

"Oh, it's because I've had diarrhea and was very sick," he answered.

"How strange. When you left this morning you were healthy and strong and now you seem so feeble."

The man lied. "Yes, it was a very sudden illness."

"And there's that bad smell you used to have."

"Yes, it must be the smell of the mountain or maybe even the sickness itself."

The woman did not understand the problem, but went on tending to him as before. When he had recovered from his poor state, the man began to fulfill his promise to work diligently to support her. He even learned not to yearn for distant things, but to like what he had: his wife, his land, his people.

The Vulture
and the Sparrow Hawk

On a certain day the vulture and the sparrow hawk, both very hungry and voracious, contemplated an old horse who looked more dead than alive, stretched out on the green grass napping.

As they stared, a gnawing indecision began to devour them since the mound of bones covered with worn hide gave off a certain furtive aroma that roused their appetites and tormented them.

For a long time they watched, unsure if it were alive or if it were dead. Since the old nag gave no sign of moving, the vulture, most blind when most hungry and determined to get the first mouthful, approached, tottering with pleasure.

The tired hawk, that great observer, sat in the tree and shouted, "Alive...! Alive! It's alive all right!"

The foolish vulture blurted out, "Dead, dead! It's dead, it's dead."

And since his hunger was stronger than his will, the vulture threw himself on the prey without thinking, sinking his curved knife of a beak beneath the tail of the sleeping and defenseless old nag who had lain down there never suspecting evil.

The horse, upon feeling himself being butchered, rose up and became a fearsome beast, unleashing like lightning a tremendous kick. It struck the target dead center — smack on the dizzy head of the crazy butcher.

The sparrow hawk futilely warned his comrade, shouting in desperation, "Alive, alive! It's alive!"

And the vulture, almost dead, replied, "Yes, oh yes! Oh yes! I was a fool. He was not dead."

The hawk with great care flew around the bloody scene, giving thanks to heaven that he had been spared the fate of his stubborn and dense comrade.

And there below, the sad vulture moaned, ready to collapse into the arms of death.

Settling down at the vulture's side, the sparrow hawk tried to console him.

"My friend, I'm very sorry about your fate, but blame no one for your own foolishness. If your hour has come, die in peace because many will learn from your example to be wiser and more cautious."

The vulture, seeing himself alone and desolate, began to wail, condemning his own craziness.

"A nag has brought my life to its end! But why torture myself if it's all over anyhow?"

And so with this sad and profound thought the vulture closed his glassy eyes and murmured, "Adiós life, adiós world."

The Buzzard and the Dove

There was once a wise old buzzard who found himself falling in love with a beautiful dove. The hand of heaven moved him. He thought long and hard about his wrinkled head, his heavy beak. Still, remembering that necessity sometimes wears a dog's face and "love has no boundaries," the lovesick buzzard fixed himself up as best he could and gallantly went out to find the dove.

When he saw the dove, she seemed even more beautiful than ever, and the buzzard stood back in awe. With all his heart he wanted to run to her, but his heavy feet refused to move. He began to doubt himself. Finally, he made up his mind and spoke out:

"Oh you divine princess, my lovely dove, I beg you, listen to what I ask. With great pain, with tears and pleas, I am your humble admirer and very proud to declare to you my tenderest love."

The dove, surprised by such sudden praise, answered: "What are you saying? Are you crazy? None of your fellow hoarse-throats have ever been so brash! You are asking for my hand, you? Such worthless love from such trash."

The buzzard had already said too much to be silenced by her insulting behavior. With gentlemanly courtesy he responded: "Forgive me, precious one, if I offend you.

you. But for a long time I have not lived in peace, thinking of nothing but you. And so my fair damsel, give me your compassion when I come to kneel at your feet and ask out of all love and submission that you join me in Christian marriage. That's all I'm asking."

But the dove, shocked by such impudence, answered in a harsh and merciless voice: "Without doubt you're drunk or crazy, you loathesome buzzard. Once and for all, before I lose my patience, I'm telling you a hundred times, I hate you. And don't ever bother me again!"

The lover wanted to continue his amorous arguments, but the dove did not want to hear any more drivel and gave him the cold shoulder.

She left the buzzard stunned and crestfallen, without spirit, without hope of winning her, muttering to heaven: "I was born humble and I'll die humble, the unluckiest creature on earth. I might as well die now and take along my fine feelings, for I live sad, poor and disgraced."

A long time passed, but the buzzard could not forget his love. Once more in his heart, a great passion blossomed for that princess who was the source of his misery.

Convinced that he could win his treasure by force of endurance and sacrifice, he scrubbed and scraped and combed and brushed. With a slow and tired step he set out to find the dove. He was sure that this time luck would not fail him and that his only duty was to fight to the death for his ideal, even if fighting for the impossible.

He caught the dove off guard when he returned to deliver his new inspiration. Like an eloquent courtier he addressed his love: "Señorita Paloma, forgive my awkwardness, but the impulses of my suffering and lovestruck heart bring me again to ask you at least for your friendship."

The dove, so proud of her beauty, interrupted his plea. With a vengeful fury she cut his fine sentiments to shreds with these words: "Oh it's you again, stupid beast. Chish, you pig. I'm telling you, I don't love you. Now get out of here before your smell offends me. Just seeing you brood scares me. What's more, the way you walk and sway is foolish and ugly."

The buzzard tried to defend himself as best he could. His eyes were filling with tears, his voice trembled. He summoned all his forces to explain to his loved one his peculiar, sad situation: "Beautiful little dove, don't judge me poorly. This smell I give off is valuable perfume. The suit I wear is my most serviceable finery. This distinct walk is how they taught me to march. So as you see, I'm not just anyone, as I appear to be, but someone ready to be received like a lieutenant or a colonel."

His explanation amused the dove. She laughed.

"Heee, heee. You call that smell from your beak perfume? And you call the disgusting color of your wings finery?"

The buzzard replied: "Señorita, instead of looking at my dress, look at the courage of my person. If you are descended from another line, don't make fun of my words or the color of my plumage."

The dove laughed again.

"Heee, heee, heee. You and your hoarse speeches. And what will you tell me about your dusty legs. That you spent a fortune to rent those stockings?"

99

The buzzard continued: "Fine little lady, I wouldn't have believed you were so cold as to discriminate against me like this. Be my condition what it may, my own dignity sustains me and I swear that if I was your suitor, it was because I did not know what a violent and prejudiced mind you have."

The haughty dove went on listing an infinity of faults in her suitor until she got tired. She took her leave saying: "Enough. Leave me alone. Go back to your own kind, you insolent brute."

The buzzard stepped back, brooding, and made way for some "authorities" who approached just then on their routine rounds. He wiped his teary eyes and grew curious about what was going on. First one official began a passionate speech, exalting things he had probably never seen: "And I, the leader of the campaign against pollution am proud to deliver this important award to our lovely dove in honor of her valuable participation in the animal plan for a clean world."

The buzzard, in a dark corner, watched the ceremony and wanted to speak out, but he knew that no one would listen. He looked at his claws and felt his beak. He had worked so hard against pollution and had never been recognized for his efforts. Instead, she who never stained her beak or her feathers was carrying away the honors. *Caramba*, what an injustice. So the buzzard started on his way home.

Meanwhile the decorated dove climbed the branches of a tall tree so that all could see her, so that everyone could applaud her. It was then that among the thick branches they heard a sudden noise. A hawk had plunged down and snatched the beautiful wild dove in its talons. This all happened so fast that the only thing those present saw were some feathers that fell as if waving goodbye to her grieving suitor.

Then seeing that everything was over, the crestfallen buzzard beat his way upward on slow wings and went across the sky doubting, crying and thinking: "What a fool I am to stay captive in this great valley of sorrows. Why not live like before, far from hatred and rancor and free of all these sorry tricks?"

The Possum and the Jaguar

The mother of the small possum told her son, "I think it's time that you went out and found someone to be your godfather." So it was that the little possum went out to search for a godfather. First he headed for the jaguar's lair. The jaguar came to attention thinking that this would be an easy meal. The possum, however, quickly shouted out the purpose of his visit. "Señor Jaguar, excuse me for bothering you, but the only thing I want is to ask if you would like to be my godfather."

"Ah, so you want me to be your godfather?" the jaguar asked.

"Yes," the possum replied.

"Very well, if that's what you want, then that's how it will be. Tomorrow I'll come for you so that we can go out and eat," the jaguar said.

"Very good, Godfather. I will be ready and waiting in the morning."

The next day the jaguar arrived at the possum's house and announced, "I have come to see my godson."

"Of course," the mother said. "Come in. He's waiting for you."

So the possum went with his godfather to the plain where there was a little fountain or "eye of the water." There other animals came to drink. Then the jaguar told the possum, "Get up in this tree and when I shout 'now there's meat', you should come quickly to find me."

"Very good, I'll do it, Godfather," said the possum and hid himself among the limbs of the tree.

At noon the thirsty cattle began to come down the hills to the spring, and the last to arrive was a black bull.

"Now I will procure some food for my godson," said the jaguar. So while the bull was drinking the jaguar leaped out of his hiding place and attacked. He felled the bull in the mud at the edge of the spring. When the meal was ready the jaguar shouted, "Godson, come quickly. "Eat all that you want, dear godson. There is plenty of meat," the jaguar said.

The possum began to eat, but he could hardly finish a mouthful.

"Eat, eat, my godson. Don't waste the food we now have so abundantly," the jaguar said.

"Thank you godfather, but my stomach is very small and I cannot eat much," the possum answered.

The jaguar ate all that he could and left part of the kill for other animals.

As they were leaving his godson said, "Many thanks godfather, now it is my turn to invite you to a banquet as you have invited me."

On the day of the invitation the jaguar arrived at his godson's house. This time the possum was ready to provide the food for the banquet, and the jaguar accompanied his godson in search of meat. The possum headed toward a little village where some laborers had chickens and turkeys in their pens. They paused at the edge of the village to wait until everyone went to sleep. At midnight the possum entered a pen to hunt. One by

one he was carrying off the chickens and turkeys for his godfather to eat. The jaguar said he was still hungry, so the possum returned to the pen to capture more hens. This time the hens made a great racket and woke up their owners who came out with dogs, sticks and machetes, ready to chase those who were ravaging the hen house. They searched the plain with flaming pine torches but found nothing.

A few days later the little possum said to his mother, "Come with me to eat, Mama. I know how my godfather got very good meat and I will do the same."

His mother went with him to the scene of the hunt.

"Climb up that tree while I hide in the bushes at the side of the spring. When I shout, 'Now there is meat' I want you to come quickly.' "

In this manner the possum hid himself in the same place from which his godfather had ambushed his prey. At noon the cattle began to come down from the hill to drink before they took their rest. In a little while a single bull also came down. While the bull drank water the possum leaped upon him in the same way his godfather had done. But the bull was not frightened and simply began to shake himself to get rid of this tickling on his shoulder. As he shook himself he hurled the possum into the air. He landed and stuck in the mud. Unable to get out, the possum called to his mother for help.

"Come here, Mama. Now there is meat" he shouted. His mother jumped to the ground thinking the meat was now ready. When she got to the spring she discovered her son almost dead, and she leaped to his rescue. But she too got trapped in the mire where it is said the two sadly died.

The Lazy Man

Once upon a time a lazy man lived with his wife on a farm in the mountains. After the rains came and it was time for planting, the wife went to look for seeds. She gave them to her husband to plant corn in the field. The man went every day to work, so it's said, but in reality he was going to sleep the whole day beneath the shade of the trees.

One day the man poked a hole and put all the seeds in it. Then, after sleeping as usual, he returned home to continue resting. All the while the wife thought her husband was a very good worker.

After some months when the corn plants in the fields of other workers began to form ears the wife asked if the plants in her husband's field were also forming ears.

"There are no ears yet. We'll have to wait a few more weeks," he answered.

Two weeks later the wife asked again, "Are there ears in the cornfield yet?"

The man insisted again that they would have to wait a few weeks. Tired of waiting, she followed his footsteps to see with her own eyes what he was talking about. The man realized she was following him and tried to fool her. "Where is our field?" she asked.

Instead of telling his wife that he had not planted the field, he showed her someone else's field.

"This is our field, but I'll ask you to stay out of it, and I will bring some ears home so we can eat."

His wife refused. "If this is our field, I cannot resist cutting some ears of corn," she said and walked among the plants. "What a beautiful field! What big stalks!" While she exclaimed how beautiful the field was, the giant who owned the field came running. The husband ran away while the wife continued contemplating the crop."

"What are you doing in my field? Thieves!" shouted the enraged giant. And since the husband had run away, the giant took the wife captive and held her in a cave in the mountains. Crying all the way, the husband returned home.

As he passed a meadow the jaguar stepped out to meet him and asked, "Why are you crying, fellow?"

"The giant has taken my wife and that is why I am sad," the man answered.

The jaguar laughed. "So you are afraid of this giant. Let me see him. I will make him return your wife."

The jaguar went to the cave where the giant lived. He knocked on the stone that served as a door. "Is anyone at home?" he asked.

The giant came out and said, "What is it you want?"

"I want you to free the woman whom you have captive here. If you don't do it, we will fight right here until I have beaten you," the jaguar said.

The giant became furious and faced off against the jaguar. The jaguar threw himself on the giant, raking his stomach with his claws. But at the same time the giant grabbed the jaguar's paws, breaking his claws. The jaguar fell down, defeated.

The husband continued crying for his wife. After a little while a mule came by and asked him, "Why are you crying, fellow?"

"I am sad because the giant has carried off my wife to a cave, and he doesn't want to return her."

The mule laughed. "Come with me. I will rescue your wife from this giant." So they arrived at the giant's cave. The mule knocked on the stone at the front of the cave.

The giant came to the door and asked, "What do you want?"

"Return to me the wife of this poor man," the mule demanded.

The giant came out into the open very angry. The mule began to run around crazily, trying to fell the giant with various kicks to the left and to the right. One time the mule delivered a blow to the giant's backside. It made him stumble but he did not fall down. Very irritated, the giant grabbed the mule by the ears and threw him far away. When the man saw the mule defeated, he began to cry inconsolably.

Along the road he met a very bold cow who asked him, "Why are you crying?"

"The giant has stolen my wife. That's why I am crying."

"Well, stop crying because I am going to help you rescue your wife," the cow offered. And so they went to the giant's cave, where the cow ordered the giant to set the woman free. The giant got very mad and came out fighting fiercely. The cow tried to impale him on her horns, but he defended himself. He grabbed the horns and with extraordinary force tore them out. Saddened by the defeat of his third friend, the man continued on his way crying.

A rabbit stepped into the path and asked, "Why are you crying, fellow?"

"I cry because the giant has robbed me of my wife," he replied.

"It seems strange to me that you are afraid of the giant since as you see, I am very small, but I am not afraid of any two-legs."

"That's what you say because you have not seen him. Many animals bigger than you have faced him, but they were all defeated and killed."

"Don't worry. First I want you to help me look for a gourd." The rabbit went in search of all kinds of wasps, especially the most aggressive and poisonous. When he had gathered the wasps, the rabbit set off to challenge the giant.

"Señor giant," he shouted, "I order you to return this man's wife. If you don't do it, then you will have to suffer the consequences."

The giant came out of his cave, furious. But he was surprised to see the size of the one who insulted him so boldly. "Ah, you are very small and I would crush you quickly. It is better for you to go away before I tear you apart with my hands," the giant growled.

"I may be very small, but I am able to conquer you right here if you don't do what I say," insisted the rabbit.

Then the giant attacked. When he came close the rabbit uncorked the gourd and the wasps streamed out. The giant, unable to defend himself, swatted crazily while the wasps attacked and buried their stingers without mercy. Tired of fighting, the giant fled down a nearby ravine pursued closely by the tireless buzzing wasps.

This is how the man was able to recover his wife, and he gave thanks to the rabbit who had defeated the giant with the help of the wasps.

But this is not the end because the rabbit demanded, "Now I want you to buy black wax and make a rabbit that looks like me. Put a gourd in the hands of this wax rabbit and plant it at the entrance of the giant's cave." And so they did it.

After several months of absence the giant wanted to return to his cave, but when he saw the rabbit there at the entrance with his gourd of wasps, he fled again, never to return.

The Great Jaguar

Long ago there was an old man who had several head of cattle widely scattered on the pastures of *Huntah* but, since these regions were very mountainous at that time, the man always went to look for his herds accompanied by his hunting dogs.

One time when the man was walking through those mountains, his three dogs began to bark at the foot of a tree. He went to see what the dogs were after. Upon seeing that it was a fierce jaguar his dogs had treed, he decided to call them off the hunt. The man knew how dangerous it was to confront such a wild animal.

The old man was about to leave the area when a young campesino appeared and asked, "Señor, what are your dogs chasing?"

"My dogs have treed a jaguar. This is a very dangerous beast and it's better that we leave."

"Have no fear. I believe today we shall eat meat," said the campesino.

"Aha, if you believe you are sufficiently quick to defend yourself, then go take a look," the old man told him.

"All right, let's go hunting. Come along with me and don't worry," the young man said. He prepared a good rope for his use.

As they approached the jaguar, he prepared for his attack. In this moment the jaguar threw himself upon the old man instead of on the young worker. When the young man saw how furiously the jaguar attacked, he hid himself. Meanwhile the old man, with extraordinary skill with the machete began to fight the beast. Fortunately the dogs also began to attack the jaguar, and this gave the old man the chance to deliver well aimed blows. The old man and the dogs continued fighting the beast until he managed to deliver a deadly blow to the head. With this the jaguar fell to the ground and the three dogs moved in. Soon the jaguar gave up and died.

"Wow! Is it already dead?" shouted the young man from his hiding place.

"Yes, come here and look," replied the old man, his blood still boiling from the fight.

The young man was afraid to come out from his hiding place because the old man was still swinging the machete furiously. After a long while the old man called the young man again. "Hey, come here and take a look. Don't be afraid."

"Don't hurt me, please, señor," shouted the young campesino.

"No. Come with me. My blood has cooled and my nerves have returned to normal," the old man said.

The young man approached, saying, "Señor, I hope that nothing has happened to you."

"To me — nothing. But I only want to tell you that if at some time you find this kind of animal, don't dare to confront it, because it is not easily defeated."

So said the old man, counseling the young man to avoid unnecessary problems and dangers. If they escaped that adventure with their lives, it was thanks to the fierceness of the hunting dogs, and above all to the bravery of this old campesino.

The Skunk and the Rabbit

Once upon a time a skunk who had no family or friends went into the mountains to look for a friend.

"I am going to look for friendship," he said. "I know that I will find someone who wants to give me his friendship."

The skunk wandered around the mountain, and suddenly he met a rabbit whose ears went up when he saw the skunk approaching.

"What are you doing here, rabbit?" asked the skunk.

"I am looking for sprouts to eat," the rabbit answered.

Then the skunk proposed, "Would you like to be my friend?"

"Yes, of course," the rabbit said. "The only problem is that you do not know how to run as fast as I do. If there were some danger, it would quickly catch you. But when there is danger, I immediately lift my ears and begin to run quickly," the rabbit said.

"Don't worry. I know that I cannot race, but also I have a powerful weapon that can repel any danger," the skunk said.

"Where do you have this weapon?" the rabbit asked.

"I carry it here beneath my tail," the skunk said.

"Very well," said the rabbit. "We will be friends, but you ought to shoot only when it is necessary."

With the friendship treaty made, the two friends set out to walk among a campesino's planted fields. The rabbit decided to remain among the green shoots of sweet potatoes while the skunk went around in the field of peanuts. The skunk was busy eating when the owner of the garden arrived and chased him out. He ran toward the place where the rabbit was eating.

At that time the rabbit was surprised by the coyote who wanted to eat him. The skunk arrived in time and quickly hid himself in a hole under a rock. "Shall I eat you today, Señor rabbit?" the coyote said.

"No, don't eat me because I am very small. But there under that rock there is a bigger animal that will fill your stomach."

"Let's go quickly," the coyote said.

The two of them went to the place where the skunk had hidden, prepared to defend himself as he had promised the rabbit. Since the coyote was hungry, he was eager to get the first bite with his long, sharp teeth. He was about to bite the skunk's back when the skunk let loose his stinking "shot." When the coyote felt that unexpected attack, he was almost blinded and began to roll around desperately, trying to free himself from the unbearable stench.

While the coyote rolled around on the ground the two friends fled quickly and hid under another rock far away. After a while the coyote found them again. This time he was ready to eat both of them right where they were. "Finally I have found you," the coyote said. "Now I will make a banquet of you."

The rabbit and the skunk were afraid, but then, the skunk prepared again for the attack.

"Friend rabbit," he said, "hold your nose because I am going to fire." And so he lifted the tail and tried, but unfortunately he could not get off his "shot."

"Friend rabbit," he said, "I have no more ammunition. We are lost!"

The rabbit began to tremble. He could not get out of the hole where they had hidden. So it was that the coyote finally defeated the rabbit in spite of many previous failures.

The Old Ones' Friendship: the Dog, the Jaguar, and the Coyote

This was an old jaguar, very old. He was wandering through the mountains, unable to catch any food. The younger jaguars had thrown him out of their group because now the old one had lost his hunting skills. While climbing up a hill he met a dog. The dog was also old, very old.

The jaguar asked, "And you, dog, what are you doing here?"

"Ah well, they have expelled me from my group. The young dogs said, 'Let this old dog leave us since we do not need him.' And so it is that I am left to wander on my own through the mountains. As you can see, they have reviled me and thrown me out of the place where I used to hunt when I was younger and stronger."

"It seems to me that the two of us are in the same situation," said the jaguar. "They have reviled me, too, and thrown me out of my group and the place where I used to hunt when I was younger and stronger."

"Ah well, then we shall be companions. Surely we must be very old for them to cast us out," said the dog, trying to extend his friendship to the jaguar.

The jaguar was pleased and suggested, "Let's travel together. What I hunt we will share. And what you hunt, too, will be for both of us. Only then will we be able to survive on this mountain."

"So it is," said the dog. "We'll stay together because now we are very old, and we need one another."

"This is good," said the jaguar. "It was great luck that we met under these circumstances. We will join forces from today on."

As they roamed about, they met the coyote.

They asked, "Well, what are you doing here, Señor Coyote?"

"My story is very sad," the coyote said. "My group has refused to let me stay with them. In spite of the fact that I feel young, they said that I'm very old and must leave. They threw me out from the place where I was used to filling my mouth every day. So it's in these sad circumstances that you find me," the coyote said.

"What a coincidence. We too have been thrown out of our groups because they think we are too old and have lost our hunting skills. Now that we've met, we've made a pact. If one of us finds something to eat, he will share it with the other. Do you want to join us?" asked the jaguar.

The dog added, "We'll join forces, not only to eat but also to defend ourselves. Though we may be very old, together we'll always be able to defend ourselves against danger."

"Yes, I want to join you," the coyote said. "I know that the three of us are very old, and we ought to join forces from today on.

So they all agreed and continued on their way.

As they walked along the trail, feeling very hungry, the coyote found a piece of bread. He wanted to gobble it up, but his friends reminded him that they all ought to share the meal. Since the piece of bread was very small and would not feed everyone, they began to consider the best way to decide who was going to be the lucky one who would eat the piece of bread. Then the jaguar made a proposal.

"We ought to tell how old each of us is, and the oldest of the three can eat the bread."

They began to tell their ages.

"Señor dog, can you tell us truthfully — don't lie now — how old you are?"

"I am very very old," the dog said. "I am one of those who has been walking the earth since ancient times — since the time when it was said that a very wise man would arrive in the world to prophesy. I have been living since then, since before all time."

"Ah, you are not very old then. What you have told us is very recent," said the jaguar. "Now take me. A long, very long time ago, I first saw the light of the sun. I'm the one who first set foot in paradise, long, long ago."

"That too is very recent," said the dog. "I believe that I am the oldest. I even remember crossing over the sea, I am the oldest of the three."

"But if you say that you were born when the wise man came to prophesy, then I am the oldest, because I was born before that and even travelled in the Ark," insisted the jaguar.

While those two had a hot debate trying to prove which one was older, the hungry coyote took advantage of the confusion and swallowed the piece of bread.

119

The discussion continued. "Perhaps we're both the same age," proposed the dog. "But the two of us have talked a lot. Now let's ask the coyote if he is older than the two of us. So far he's said nothing."

So they asked the coyote, "Señor coyote — would you tell us how old you are?"

"Truthfully, I do not feel as old as you," responded the coyote.

"If you're not really old, why do you walk along with us? You should be with the others your age," they told him.

"Well, they have thrown me out, and since I am hungry, I joined you."

"Then you cannot compete for the piece of bread," they advised him.

"What piece of bread?" the coyote asked, pretending surprise.

Then the jaguar and the dog realized that while they were arguing the coyote had devoured the bread without saying a word.

"Señor coyote, you cannot join us because you don't know how to behave among friends and you don't even respect the rules that should govern our unity."

So the coyote was thrown out again. The dog and the jaguar continued on their way always discussing their age and it seems that in the end they came to an agreement. The two seemed to remember riding in the Ark many, very many years ago. And so they proved to themselves that they were the oldest animals on the earth.

Notes:

Images shown in this collection are described in greater detail in:
> *The Maya Book of the Dead* by F. Robicsek and D. Hales,
> published by The University of Virginia Art Museum, 1981.
> *Lords of the Underworld* by M. Coe and Kerr, published by
> Art Museum Princeton University, 1978.
> *Old Gods and Young Heroes* by M. Coe, published by Israel
> Museum/Bradock Press, 1982.

Most of the images are taken from ceramic vessels from the mid-part of the Late Classic Maya Period at the turn of the eighth century. Most are in the Codex Style Site A. It was originally thought that all were from the Calakmul area of Southern Campeche but studies show they are from other regions as well, including El Peru from Southern Campeche and 2 areas near the Guatemalan-Belize Border.

Insofar as the colors were not maintained during the years they were buried, we (the publishers and the author) acknowledge that we have taken liberties in assigning colors to the images. We have, however, tried to use colors that are reasonably accurate.

page 17   A layered package (possibly a Codex) with a bouquet or whisk of quetzal feathers and a round object, probably a shell on top is shown on left. To the right are an ancient bearded god and a monster-headed deity both holding vases.

page 28   The mythological combination of a water bird and harpy eagle with a snake around its elongated neck is perched on the body of a dead human. Due to erosion of the glyphs it cannot be identified.

page 32   The Killer Bat is holding a bowl with Iconic Triad of hand, eye and long bone. Above the bat is (T526 Caban grapheme) the earth, which suggests that the event portrayed took place in a cave or in the Underworld.

page 43   Dancing Animal Dieties — A polychrome vase from Northern Peten or Southern Campeche, portraying the Spider Monkey.

page 50   The crouching jaguar dog, with hound-like ears, is a super-natural beast distinguished from other dog-like deities on Maya ceramics which have short, torn ears.

page 55   An unidentified toad is shown with T1 symbols affixed to its back just below the unusual spinal fin.

page 63   From the Chama Region, Chixoy River, Guatemala. This vase is the best known and most often copied by forgers of all the classic maya vases. The scene may depict a meeting between merchants as this figure has been identified as "God M, Ek Chuah, the black god of traveling merchants."

page 81   The Water Lily Jaguar is wearing a sacrificial scarf. He has glyphic elements for water affixed to his head, elbow and back.

page 84   Old God L is pictured in a headdress topped by a Muan-bird, a screech owl of ill-omen. God L is seated on his throne surrounded by harem ladies in an underworld palace.

page 88   A toad is holding a macabre Triad bowl of hand, long bone, and disembodied eye. The toad wears a water lily headdress on which a fish is nibbling.

Page 96   A spotted Muan-bird holds the severed head of the Jaguar God of the Underworld in its beak.

page 104   The Water Lily Jaguar has a sacrificial scarf about his shoulders. He is identified as GIII of the Palenque Triad of Gods. It appears to be destined for decapitation as indicated by the scarf. Behind the Water Lily Jaguar, the heads of a young musician protrudes from the mouth of a Deer Dragon.